THIS BOOK BELONGS TO:

little man Fraser

enjoy it when you get bigger!

♡ gina

Gyo Fujikawa's A to Z PICTURE BOOK

STERLING

New York / London
www.sterlingpublishing.com/kids

STERLING and the distinctive Sterling logo are registered trademarks of Sterling Publishing Co., Inc.

Library of Congress Cataloging-in-Publication Data

Fujikawa, Gyo.
  Gyo Fujikawa's A to Z picture book / Gyo Fujikawa.
    p. cm.
  Originally published by: Grosset & Dunlap, 1974.
  ISBN 978-1-4027-6818-7 (hc-pld)
  1. English language--Alphabet--Juvenile literature. 2. Alphabet books. 3. Vocabulary--Juvenile literature. I. Title. II. Title: A to Z picture book.
  PE1155.F85 2010
  [E]--dc22

                    2010003450

Lot #: 10 9 8 7 6 5 4 3 2 1
06/10
Published in 2010 by Sterling Publishing Co., Inc.
387 Park Avenue South, New York, NY 10016
By arrangement with J.B. Communications, Inc., and Ronald K. Fujikawa.
Text and illustrations © 2007 by The Gyo Fujikawa Copyright Trust.
Originally published by Grosset & Dunlap in 1974
Distributed in Canada by Sterling Publishing
c/o Canadian Manda Group, 165 Dufferin Street
Toronto, Ontario, Canada M6K 3H6
Distributed in the United Kingdom by GMC Distribution Services
Castle Place, 166 High Street, Lewes, East Sussex, England BN7 1XU
Distributed in Australia by Capricorn Link (Australia) Pty. Ltd.
P.O. Box 704, Windsor, NSW 2756, Australia

Sterling ISBN 978-1-4027-6818-7

For information about custom editions, special sales, premium and corporate purchases, please contact Sterling Special Sales Department at 800-805-5489 or specialsales@sterlingpublishing.com.

Acorn

Alligator

Anchor

Amaryllis

Automobile

Argument

Airplane

Artist

Anger

Agreement

Eat an apple before going to bed—
make the doctor beg for bread.

Armadillo

a

A is for alone,
    all by myself . . .
    Hi, there, frog!
Can I play with you?

Bugle

Bobolink

Butterfly

Bashful

Ball

Bow

Bonnet

Bunny

Bell

Bib

Bottle

Bear

Black eye

Boat

Banana

Blackberries

Boots

Button

Balloon

Bicycle

Boxes

Bags

Bone

Belly button

Bread

Barrel

Basket

Bee

Bug

Buttercup

Bed

Bye-bye

B is for busy babies!

Clover

Candy

Chipmunk

Clown

Cone

Chicken

Chicks

Crown

Cow

Chocolate cake

Calf

Chair

Cuckoo clock

Chickadee

Charlie is cold.

Clara is crawling.

Cat and copycat

Camel

Crybaby

Crab

Caterpillar

Cactus

Cheese

C is for city!

D

Daisy

Deer

Dormouse

Dragonfly

Doctor

Doll

Dogs

Dachsund

Duck and ducklings

Dove

Dolphin

Diver

Doghouse

Daffodil

David digs.

Dandelion

D is for dreams,
    all kinds of dreams,

dangerous   and delicious ones . . .

dreadful,   delightful,   and disgusting ones!

Edelweiss

Emma cleans her ears.

Eye

Feather

Elf

Elephant

Eskimo

Edward is eating.

Eggs

Frog

Furry friends

Fox

Fig

Fish

Figleaf

Flamingo

Forget-me-not

Fearless Freddie

F is for
friends,
fairies,
flowers,
fish,
and frogs.

Gull

Gossip

Grapes

Giraffe

Geranium

May the
garland of
friendship
be ever
green.

Goose

Ginny
is a
giggler.

Hummingbird

Halo

Harp

House

Hatchet

Hammer

Hollyhocks

Horse

Home Sweet Home

h

Hungry Henry

Happy Harold

Hamburger

Hot dog

H is for Halloween!

Icebergs

Iron

Igloo

Icing

Ibis

Iris

Ice cream

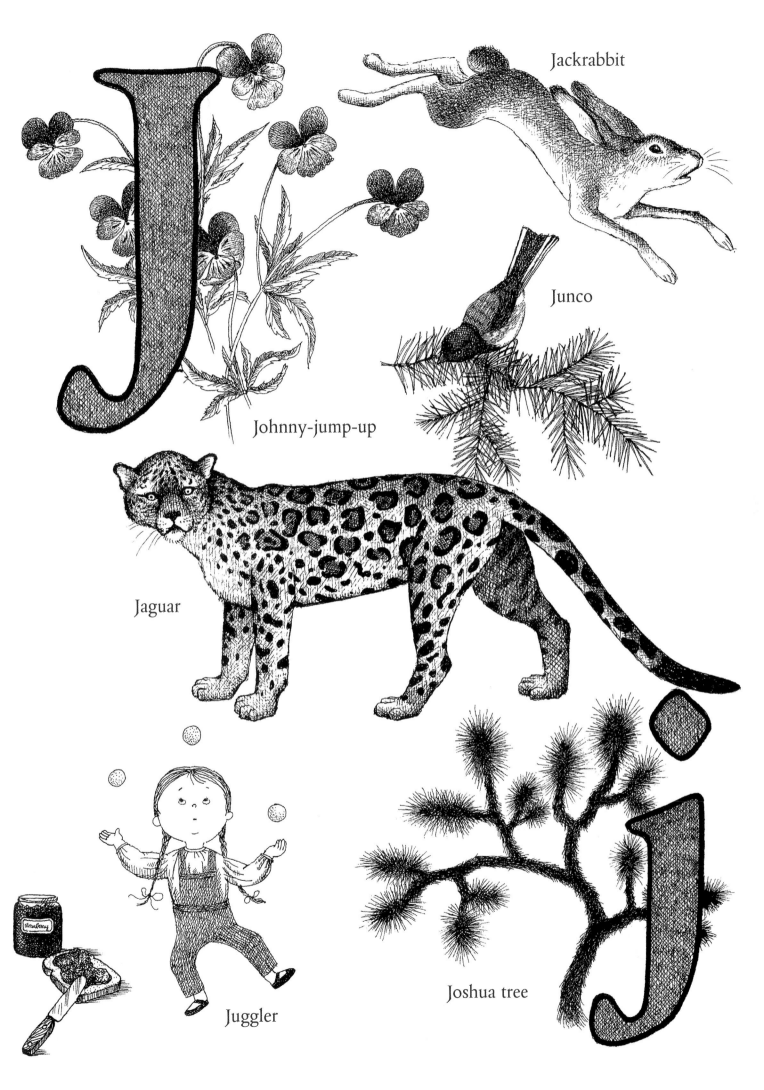

Jackrabbit

Junco

Johnny-jump-up

Jaguar

Juggler

Joshua tree

J is for
jump,
jump,
jump!

K

Kookaburra

Katydid

Kenny is kowtowing.

Kangaroo

Koala

Key

Kiwi

k

Lobster

Lark

Llama

Lilies

Lizard

L is for lullaby,
        lions,
        lizards,
        lemons,
        and lambs.

L is for love,
        leopard,
        and lilies of the valley.

Moon

Monkey

Mountains

Mulberry

Mouse

Mint

Melon

Meow

Mitten

Muffler

Muff

Morning glory

Moo goo gai pan

Mockingbord

Mackerel

Moose

Milk

Marigold

Mushrooms

m

M is for
   my mean
   and marvelous
   monsters.

Nest

Newt

Nene

Nasturtium

Nurse

Nautilus

Necklace

Nightingale

Nuts

Nestlings

N is for numbers!

Owl

Orange

Ostrich

Octopus

Opossum

Otter

Orchid

Onions

P

Plum pudding

Parrot

Pumpkin pie

Pig

Potato

Pear

Panda

Peach

Peter pouts.

Puppy

Pansies

P is for
pigeon,
penguin,
peacock,
puddle,
and polliwogs.

Queue

Queen

Quail

Queen Anne's lace

Quiet!

Quill

Quarrel

Quintuplets

q

Robin

Rose

Raccoon

Rhinoceros

Rolling pin

Raspberries

Rat

R is for rain, rain,
and lots more rain.
Stop! I say—
Enough is enough!

Shower

Sponge

Soap

Swallow

Starfish

Sandpiper

Smiling Sam swims.

Snake

Stuck-up

Seal

Shrimp

Swan

Sea horse

Snowdrops

Spaghetti

Shell

Sapsucker

Skunk

S is for sunflowers,
    squirrels,
    strawberries,
    and snails.

S is for black-eyed Susans,
    and spiders,
    and Sam the setter.

S is for summertime,
    sparrows,
    and snoozes
    in secret shelters.

Teardrops

Thimble

Thrasher

Tiger lily

Teeth

Toothbrush

Toothpaste

Towel

Tall

Toboggan

Tabby

Tramp

Tomato

Tough

Tender

Thanksgiving turkey

Tough

Tender

Thyme

Toad

t

Tugboat

Trumpet

Trout

T is for
topsy-turvy!

Tiger

Trees

Tepee

Taxicab

Tulips

Triplets

Thistles

Train

Tightrope

Trapeze

Tuba

Tow truck

Teddy bear

Teapot

Toucan

Teacup

Turtle

Up

Under

Ugly

Umbrella

Urn

Unicorn

Upside-down cake

Ukulele

Vain

Vane

Volcano

Visit

Vaccination

Be My Valentine

Valise

Violet

Vest

Violin

V is for
vegetables.

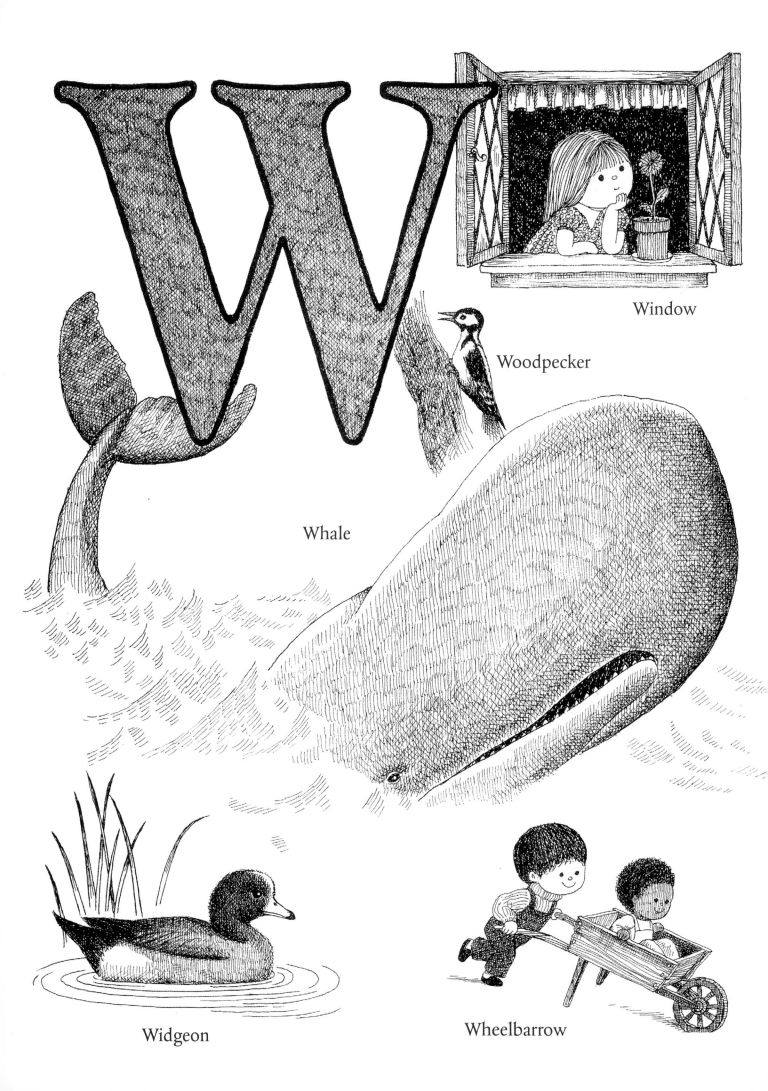

Window

Woodpecker

Whale

Widgeon

Wheelbarrow

Whip-poor-will

Walrus

Watermelon

Weeping willow

Washing   Wiping

Weasel

Wading

Water

Sweet William

W is for long wintertimes,
    the whistling wind,
    the winter wren,
    and the worm.

W is for the woodchuck too,
    warm and nestled in his bed.
    How wise to sleep away the time
    until the welcome spring!

X-ray

X marks the spot.

XXXXXX is for kisses.

X is for
railraod crossing.

Xeranthemum

Xylophone

Yak

Yoo-hoo!

Yew

Yo-yo

Yellow jacket

Yacht

Yam

Yucca

Yawn

Y is for
yuletide!

Zinnia

Zombie

Zero

Zipper

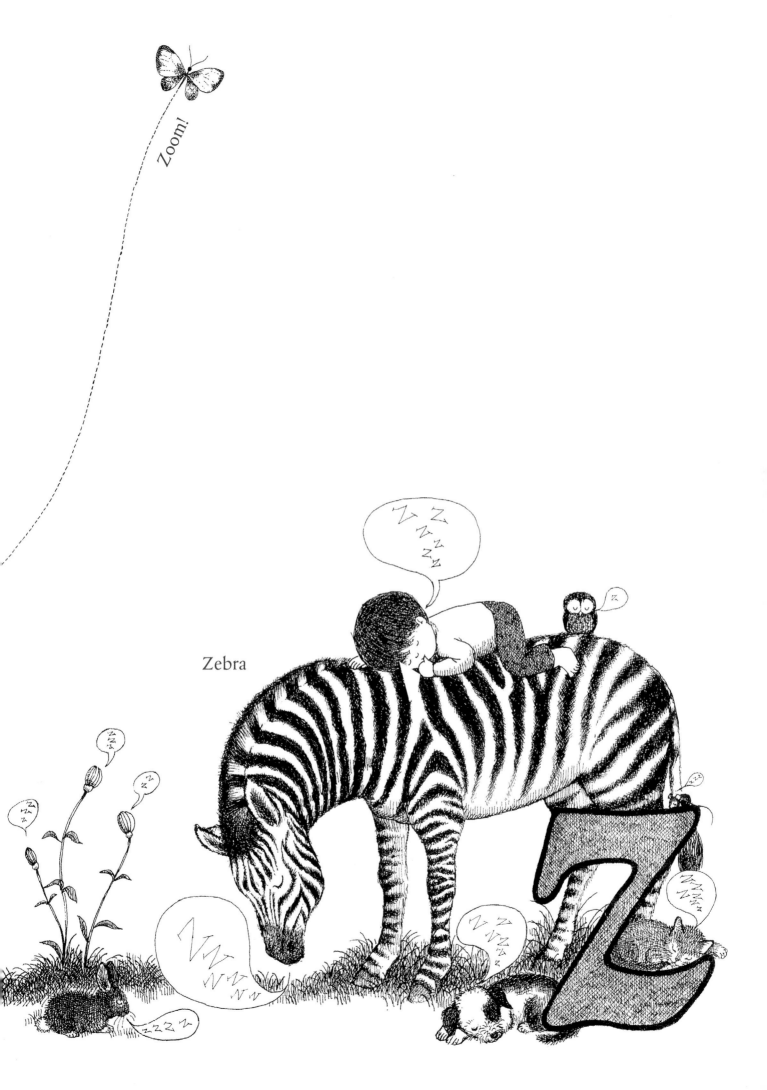

Zebra